ARMANDO ASKED, "WHY?"

Copyright © 1990 American Teacher Publications
Published by Raintree Publishers Limited Partnership
All rights reserved. No part of this book may be reproduced or utilized in any form or by any
means, electronic or mechanical, including photocopying, recording, or by any information storage
and retrieval system without permission in writing from the Publisher. Inquiries should be
addressed to Raintree Publishers, 310 West Wisconsin Avenue, Milwaukee, Wisconsin 53203.

Library of Congress number: 90-8021

Library of Congress Cataloging in Publication Data

Hulbert, Jay.
  Armando asked, "Why?" / by Jay Hulbert and Sid Kantor; illustrated by Pat Hoggan.

  (Ready-set-read)
  Summary: Armando's family are too busy to answer his questions until one day they take him to
the library, introduce him to the librarian, and find books with the answers to his questions.
  [1. Questions and answers—Fiction. 2. Libraries—Fiction. 3. Family life—Fiction.] I. Kantor, Sid.
II. Hoggan, Pat, ill. III. Title. IV. Series.
PZ7.H8755AR 1990   [E]—dc20   90-8021
ISBN 0-8172-3576-0

1 2 3 4 5 6 7 8 9   94 93 92 91 90

Armando Asked, "Why?"

by Jay Hulbert and Sid Kantor
illustrated by Pat Hoggan

Raintree Publishers
Milwaukee

Armando was always asking questions.
One Saturday, Armando asked his mother,
"Mami, why is water wet?"

"Good question, Armando," Mami said.
"But I'm too busy right now.
Let's talk about it later."

Armando asked his father,
"Papi, why is the sky so high?"

"Good question, Armando," Papi said.
"But I'm too busy right now.
Let's talk about it later."

7

Armando asked his grandmother,
"Nana, why do birds sing?"

"Good question, Armando," Nana said.
"But I'm too busy right now.
Let's talk about it later."

Armando asked his brother,
"Ricky, why is a frog green?"

"Good question, Armando," Ricky said.
"But I'm too busy right now.
Let's talk about it later."

"Why, why, why?" asked Armando.
"Why doesn't anyone answer my
questions around here?"

Everyone looked at Armando.

"It's time you got good answers to all your good questions," Papi said.

Then Mami smiled.
"I have an idea," she said.

Mami whispered to Papi. Papi smiled.

Papi whispered to Nana. Nana smiled.
Nana whispered to Ricky. Ricky smiled, too.

"Come on, Armando," Nana said.
"We're all going to the library."

"Why?" asked Armando.
"You'll see," Ricky said.

Mami brought Armando over to
meet the librarian.

Soon everyone had books—
books with answers to Armando's questions.

Armando smiled. Then he asked his family,

"Why didn't anyone think of this before?"

Sharing the Joy of Reading

Reading a book aloud to your child is just one way you can help your child experience the joy of reading. Now that you and your child have shared **Armando Asked, "Why?",** you can help your child begin to think and react as a reader by encouraging him or her to:

- Retell or reread the story with you, looking and listening for the repetition of specific letters, sounds, words, or phrases.

- Make a picture of a favorite character, event, or key concept from this book.

- Talk about his or her own ideas or feelings about the characters in this book and other things that the characters might do.

Here is an activity that you can do together to help extend your child's appreciation of this book: You and your child can visit the library together. Help your child apply for a library card, if he or she has not done so already. Does your child have a question that you are unable to answer? You might try to find the answer with the help of the librarian. The librarian can also show you the different features of the children's room, such as a reference section or a read-aloud area. Many libraries also offer a storytelling hour and other activities that might be of interest to you and your child.